Jack
and the
Beanstalk

and the giant!

For Charles, Samuel, and Emilia

Text copyright © 2015 by Nosy Crow
Illustrations copyright © 2014 by Nosy Crow
Nosy Crow and its logos are trademarks of Nosy Crow Ltd. Used under license.

First U.S. edition 2017

Library of Congress Catalog Card Number pending
ISBN 978-0-7636-9332-9

17 18 19 20 21 22 GBL 10 9 8 7 6 5 4 3 2 1

Printed in Shenzhen, Guangdong, China

This book was typeset in Clarendon.
The illustrations were created digitally.

Nosy Crow
an imprint of
Candlewick Press
99 Dover Street
Somerville, Massachusetts 02144

www.nosycrow.com
www.candlewick.com

Jack
and the
Beanstalk

illustrated by
Ed Bryan

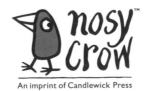

An imprint of Candlewick Press

Once upon a time, there was a boy named **Jack** who lived with his mother in a tiny little cottage. They were **very** poor.

Jack was a **good** boy, and he was very **brave**, but he didn't always think things through.

One day, Jack's mother asked her son to take their **COW** to the market. "We have nothing to eat and no money," she said. "We **have** to sell Daisy."

Jack **fed** Daisy, **brushed** her,
and put a **bell** around her neck,
then set off for the market.

Jack and Daisy had not gone
very far before they met a
strange-looking man with
a **suitcase.**

"Hello, young man," said the stranger. "What a **lovely cow** you've got! If you give her to me, you can have ten of these **magic beans.**"

Magic Beans

"How **exciting!**" Jack replied. "I'll take them!"

But when Jack got home and showed his mother the beans, she was **VERY** angry.

"I can't believe you swapped our **only cow** for these ridiculous **beans!**" she shouted.

"But they're **magic beans!**" Jack cried.
"They're not magic, you **silly** boy!" said his mom,
and she threw the beans out the window.

The next morning, when Jack woke up, he found an **enormous** beanstalk in his yard. He decided to climb up it.

Jack climbed **higher**
and **higher**
and **higher**.

The beanstalk seemed
to go on **forever!**

At last, Jack reached the **top** of the beanstalk. To his amazement, a long path led to a **huge castle** in the clouds!

Jack walked up to the castle and went inside.

Right away, a little mouse ran up to Jack. "This is the **giant's** castle," it said. "He's **scary**!"

"I'm **not** afraid of giants!" said Jack. "I'm going to have a look around."

The first room Jack found was the
kitchen, where a **cook** was
making soup. **"Please**, can
you help me make the giant's
lunch?" she asked.

Jack chopped vegetables and stirred ingredients.
Soon the soup smelled **delicious**.

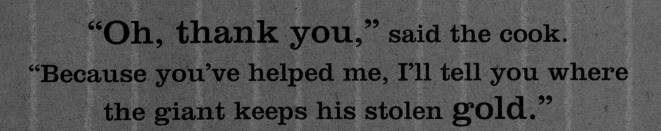

"Oh, thank you," said the cook.
"Because you've helped me, I'll tell you where
the giant keeps his stolen **gold**."

So Jack followed the cook's directions to the giant's **counting house,** where the **giant** was having his morning nap. "Whatever you do," said the mouse, **"don't** wake the giant!"

ZZZZZZ

Jack **carefully** lifted the giant's hands and took some **coins.** He stuffed them into his bag, then crept out of the room.

Jack kept exploring. Soon he found
a room where a **frog** sat by a **well.**

"**Please**, can you help me?" said the frog.
"The giant stole my **golden ball** and
threw it down this well!"

Jack lowered the **bucket** into the well, scooped up
the ball, and brought the bucket up again.
The frog **hopped** for joy.

"**Oh, thank you,**" said the frog.
"Because you've helped me, I'll tell you where
the giant keeps his stolen **magic goose.**"

So Jack went to the **goosery**, where the **giant** was sleeping after his lunch.

"One of these geese lays **golden eggs**," said the mouse. "Can you find it without waking the giant?"

Jack lifted each goose until he found a **golden egg!** He tucked the egg and the goose into his bag, then crept out of the room.

Underneath the castle, Jack found the dungeon,
where a baby dragon was locked in a cell.
"Please, can you help me?" said the dragon.
"I'm just a baby, and I want to go home to my mom!"

Jack took the **big iron key** off its hook on the wall,
turned it in the lock, and **freed** the baby dragon.

"**Oh, thank you,**" said the dragon.
"Because you've helped me, I'll tell you where
the giant keeps his stolen **golden harp.**"

Happy Honky-Tonk Ltd.

So Jack made his way to the **music room**, where the giant was having yet **another** nap. "**Please**, can you help me?" said the little golden harp. "I want to escape from the giant. He's so **mean**."

Jack picked up the harp, but it suddenly started to shout.

"I tricked you!" it screeched.

"I'm going to call my master now!

Master Giant,
wakey **wakey!**

This boy Jack is trying

to **take** me!"

The giant woke up and glared around him.
"Fee, fi, fo, **fum,**" he boomed.
"I can smell you! **Here I come!**"

The giant **chased** Jack through the castle.

"You may think that you're the **winner**, but I'll eat you up for **dinner!**" shouted the giant.

The giant **chased** Jack down the beanstalk.

"You can try to **run away**, but I'll eat you up **today!**" the giant yelled.

When Jack reached the ground, he grabbed
an **ax** and chopped the beanstalk down.
It toppled over with a loud **CRASH!**

The giant was **never** seen or
heard from again. And as for Jack and his mother,
they both lived **happily** ever after.

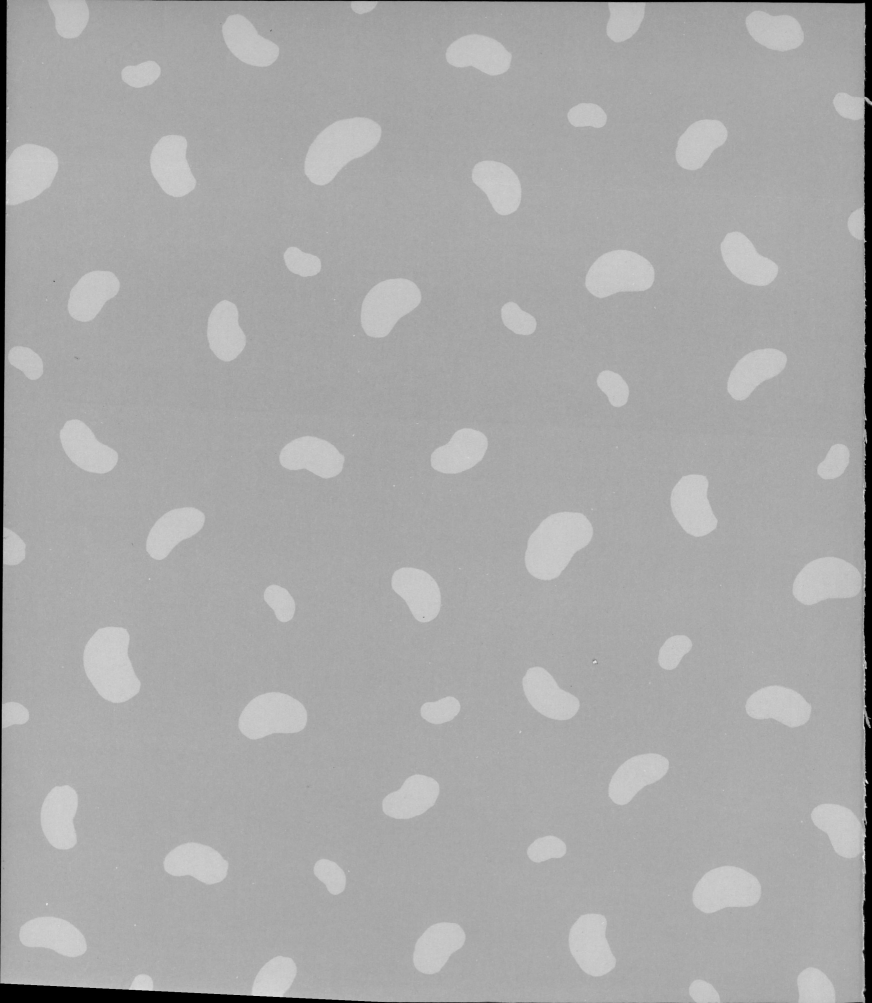